Fourth Grade Began with Betrayal

Leah Anesta

For all my children and
teachers
with love

Visit
leahanesta.com
to meet the author
and for
teacher and school resources

Chapter 1: Having Her Back

After recess, the kids walked back to the classroom in kind of a sloppy line. A couple of the boys darted over to the water fountain for a quick slurp without asking and wiped their dripping chins on the short sleeves of their t-shirts. It was a hot and muggy September afternoon, so faces were flushed and everyone was tired. Quiet reading time would be a nice chance to rest and cool off. Sarah plopped down at her desk and pulled out her new library book. She was just ready to open the cover when she saw Tracy marching up to Mrs. Armstrong's desk. Uh oh.

At first Mrs. Armstrong looked annoyed. No one was supposed to interrupt quiet reading time. But Tracy looked really determined and Sarah could tell that words were tumbling out of her mouth a mile a minute. Was she tattling? Mrs. Armstrong patted Tracy's shoulder, pointed Tracy to her desk, and called Angela out to the hallway. Everyone started glancing around the room at each other. It was quiet, but no one was reading. This was the first time since they started fourth grade last week that anyone had gotten into trouble. What would Mrs. Armstrong do? They could hear her voice but not her words. Then Angela's voice seeped through the hallway door. She sounded kind of shrieky.

"I didn't Mrs. Armstrong, I promise I didn't! Tracy's just lying to get me in trouble! Ask Sarah - she'll tell you!"

Sarah's stomach flipped and she banged her knee on the bottom of the desk. "Ow, uh oh, ow! No, no, no! Why me?" she said to herself. "There were a bunch of kids around us at recess. I'm not the only one who heard what Angela said to Tracy! Maybe she thinks that I'm the only one who'll be on her side. No, not the only one. Everyone wants to be Angela's friend. Why me? She has lots of friends." The voice in her head was her own, yet it sounded like a little kid.

Mrs. Armstrong opened the door and motioned for Tracy to go into the hallway. Whew. Then she motioned for Sarah to go too. Everyone was looking at her. She didn't know how she could tell that since she was only looking at the floor, wending her way through the maze of desks and chairs toward the door. The door seemed heavy and hard to pull open. She had to hold it with both hands as she stepped into the hallway.

Angela looked at Sarah, her eyes pleading for help. Then she looked angry, her eyes threatening "You'd better…," then pleading again. Pleading, threatening, pleading, threatening.

Sarah looked at Tracy. She just seemed stubborn, her lower lip overlapping her upper lip, her arms crossed. They never played together, even though Sarah, her mom, and her grandma lived in the basement apartment of Tracy's house. Tracy never played with any of the girls. She usually played soccer or baseball with the boys at recess.

Mrs. Armstrong looked at Sarah. Oh boy, it was like she could read her mind. Mrs. Armstrong was one of the coolest teachers. Everyone wanted to be in her class. She let all the kids help with the big aquarium and she was in charge of the science club. Her class got to do projects like make papier mache creatures and build stuff with wood and nails and hammers. She played happy music in the classroom while the kids unpacked their backpacks in the morning. And she was always, always smiling - except now.

Now she said, "Sarah, Tracy tells me that Angela said something mean to her at recess. Angela says she didn't. Please tell me what you know about this."

"Mrs. Armstrong, may I please go to the bathroom?" Sarah said.

She barely got the stall door latched and her shorts down in time. Her legs were jittery and her brains were jumbled. Angela *did* say something mean to Tracy. That was the truth. Mrs. Armstrong was counting on her to tell the truth. Sarah could tell that her teacher liked her. If she didn't tell the truth, Mrs. Armstrong might not ever like her again. But it was kind of weird that Tracy actually told. It always seemed like nothing hurt her feelings. She was tough! And she *did* act like a tomboy after all. She never wore dresses or skirts or jewelry. She challenged every boy that tried to keep her from playing sports with them, saying she could beat them any day. She would even hold up her fists and say she was ready to fight! So maybe Angela was right, maybe what she had said was true.

All three of them were silent when Sarah got back from the bathroom. All three of them were looking at her. She took a deep breath. "Angela said Tracy wants to be a real boy." (When Angela had said it, the first thing that popped into Sarah's head was, "like Pinocchio." Now it didn't sound so cute.)

Angela started shrieking again. "I did not! You liar! I only said that because she is so annoying! She's just like a boy!" She didn't say it? Or she did say it, but that was OK because it was true? Angela wasn't making sense.

Mrs. Armstrong told Tracy and Sarah to go back to quiet reading time. They heard her tell Angela that she was taking her to Principal Anesta's office.

For the rest of the day Angela was all Sarah could think about. What had she done? Last year they played at recess every day. After school and on weekends they played dress ups and gave each other fancy hairdos. They danced and lip-synced to all the new songs. And this year was going to be the best! They were best friends. Angela was Sarah's only friend. Everybody else just let her play with them because of Angela.

Sarah sat in their regular seat on the bus ride home, but Angela didn't sit next to her like usual. She sat in the seat right behind. Sarah looked down at the spot where Angela had poked a hole through the red vinyl seat with her pencil on the first day of school. She pushed her finger into the hole and pulled at it a little. Everything was ruined. She had told on her only friend - but was that wrong? Wasn't it important to be honest no matter what?

Angela began kicking the back of Sarah's seat. It didn't hurt, but it was humiliating. Then Angela started in on her, hissing right behind her ear, "It's all your fault! Principal Anesta called my parents and made me tell them everything. Now I'll be grounded for the rest of my life! YOU BETRAYED ME! You should have had my back. Why didn't you have my back?"

What did that mean?

Chapter 2: Flashback

It was rainy over the weekend, so Sarah stayed in her bedroom coloring quietly. She thought back to just before Labor Day when one of the most *significant* days came - shopping day!

Sarah had tried on all of the fancy, sparkling, and twirly outfits in her size before she chose the five she was allowed, one for each school day in the week. At the checkout counter there was a display of gem encrusted barrettes in all colors. She looked up at her mom and mouthed "pleases." Her mom held up two fingers and nodded yes. It didn't take long to find two hair clips that would go with everything since all of the dresses, skirts, and blouses were jewel colors, mostly pink or purple. Then they bought shoes for Sarah, one pair of strappy sandals with little pointy heels that her mom called "kitten heels" and one pair of sneakers. At least the sneakers were pink! After the mall, they stopped at the drugstore. Sarah wandered into the cosmetic aisles while her mom shopped for who knows what. When Sarah heard her mom call out, she grabbed the Cheeky Cherry lip gloss and matching nail polish, and a package of face gem stickers. Her mom looked at what Sarah had in her hands and just shrugged. That meant OK! Yay! Fourth grade was going to be fabulous!

At home, Sarah modeled all of her new outfits for Grandma. It was hard to tell if Grandma really liked them. She just made mm-hmm noises and said she hoped Sarah would be comfortable. She also reminded Sarah that on gym days she would have to wear the shorts and t-shirts she had worn all summer. Way to cast a cloud over the day Grandma! But of course she didn't say that. She just changed into her regular clothes and set the table for dinner. Beans and cornbread again. Grandma poured iced tea for Sarah's mother and herself, and she put a big glass of milk at Sarah's place. Sarah didn't mention the burger and fries she'd had at lunch or the hot fudge sundae that had made her sleepy on the way home. Grandma would have called it a belly full of garbage, but the way she said it would sound like "gobbage." Sarah couldn't eat more than a few bites of cornbread and a forkful of beans. She did drink down the whole glass of milk or Grandma would have fussed.

Later, getting to sleep was hard. It wasn't even dark yet. Grandma's bed, under the window against the other wall, was perfectly made with the corners tucked tight. Sarah climbed onto it and pulled the ruffled curtains closed, then jumped over to her own bed! Hmm, she hoped Grandma wouldn't notice that her bed wasn't quite as perfectly made anymore. Sarah tried to go to sleep, but all she could think about was how glamorous she looked in her new clothes. Her legs twitched a little and she kept turning from side to side. She couldn't wait for the new school year! Finally, she opened the library book that she had begun reading the night before and turned toward the wall. If Grandma came in Sarah would be able to close the book and hide it under the covers.

The book was about a girl that was really a princess but no one else knew it. She had to pass a royalty test of living with peasants and keeping her real identity a secret. If she could maintain her true royal essence while living as a peasant, she would get to go back to the castle and be queen one day. Sarah knew just how she felt. Reading was like watching a movie or dreaming. It was like being someone else.

On the first day of school, Sarah's mom helped her apply the face gems and put on some shiny dangly earrings that she kept in a blue velveteen box. She watched as Sarah carefully applied the lip gloss and nail polish. They sang "I Gotta Feeling," flashing their eyes at each other and dancing exuberantly while the nail polish dried. Sarah and her mom were great dance partners! Grandma pursed her lips when she came close for a hug and could see all the fanciness. She disapproved, that was clear. But Mom liked to see Sarah all glammed up, so Grandma wouldn't criticize out loud. On the walk to the bus stop, Sarah practiced flipping her hair back and making her earrings swing. She felt gorgeous!

The other kids stared at Sarah as they entered their classroom for the first time. She was sure they were admiring her, but somehow she felt uncomfortable. No one else had on such fancy clothes. Angela had on a really cute swingy skirt and small earrings that looked like pearls. She didn't look glamorous like Sarah. She looked elegant.

The morning passed quietly as the teacher, Mrs. Armstrong, gave out textbooks and explained the homework plans. It was so cool that everyone got a printed weekly calendar with all of the homework assignments on it. Sarah hated trying to copy down the homework from the white board. She always forgot something or wrote down the wrong pages. Mrs. Armstrong also assigned jobs for the week and Sarah got to water the plants that sat on the window sill. There were jade plants, geraniums, and marigolds. Grandma was always naming the plants they saw on their neighborhood walks, so Sarah could identify a lot of plants.

At lunch time Sarah made sure that she was the last one in the cafeteria line. That way not too many other kids heard the cafeteria lady at the cash register say "Sarah Madison, free lunch!" By the time Sarah got to the class lunch table, most of the seats near Angela were taken. A space just one spot away from the end was open, so she sat there. Climbing over the bench in her new clothes was awkward. The girl at the end of the bench was new to the school. She hadn't said a word in class and wasn't talking to anyone at the table, probably because she didn't know much English. Her name was Ilaria, pronounced "Eelahreeah". Sarah thought the name was melodic. Ilaria smiled at Sarah and Sarah smiled back. It must be hard to be new and not even know how to talk to anyone.

The cafeteria got loud as everyone chattered. But no one was talking to Sarah.

"Hey Angela," Sarah called out loudly. Now everyone looked at her. "Guess what! My mom signed me up for theater school. I get to go to acting class every Saturday and I could become a star! First I'll have to do kids' shows at the theater school, but then some talent agent might see me there and take me to Broadway!"

That got everyone's attention.

"That's great," said Angela. "My mom signed me up for theater school, too. We'll be in acting class together."

Sarah smiled and nodded her head. It was great that they would be in acting class together. They were friends. Sure. It would be great. The kids around Angela were talking and laughing, but Sarah couldn't hear what they were saying. No one was looking at Sarah anymore. She got up from the table and carried her tray to the return window. On the way back to the table her earrings jangled and her skirt swished. She bounced as she walked, making everything jangle and swish more. Some of the kids watched her. Sarah smiled at them and waved a little.

But all that was before everything changed. Before Angela wasn't her friend anymore.

Chapter 3: Getting into the Routine

Sarah stuck to the daily routines sheet that Mrs. Armstrong handed out. It was kind of weird to have your teacher tell you what to do *after* school, but Grandma said it seemed like a good plan, and she was the boss while mom was at work.

Daily Routines

1.Take a break when you get home from school. Have a snack and play outside if the weather allows.

2. Do the assigned homework, and after 40 minutes, STOP.

3. If you know ahead of time that sports, parties, or extracurricular activities will use up your homework time, get it done before the day it's assigned. No excuses!

4. Every evening: bathe, and brush your teeth.

5. Read for at least 30 minutes.

6. Sleep for 10 hours.

Mrs. Armstrong was so particular about words and phrases, like "bathe" instead of "take a bath."

She said that the words and phrases people use make an important impression on others. She also said that people think in words. Maybe, but Sarah wondered if some people thought differently, like in images, or movement, or music. How would we ever know? If people think in words, did that mean babies didn't think until they could understand words?

Maybe they didn't think, they just felt all the feelings without any words. Sarah imagined it was like floating in feelings.

But what about deaf people? How did they learn to think without hearing words? Did sign language have a different sign for every single word? It would be really hard to make a different sign as fast as hearing people speak. Sarah had seen sign language interpreters on tv, and it seemed like they didn't just sign words. They kind of acted out feelings along with the signs. Some of them were so exaggerated that Sarah giggled and tried to imitate them. It was fun! Grandma said that wasn't nice, but Sarah wasn't making fun of them. She thought the gesturing was great! It was good practice for acting class.

She was really excited about starting acting class. Even though Angela would be in the acting class too, it wouldn't be any worse than seeing her in regular class at school. Ever since *that day*, Sarah tried to look away whenever Angela cast a sour look in her direction.

Sarah fantasized about bowing on stage while a whole audience applauded her. And then, after she went off stage, they gave her a standing ovation! All of the kids would be there and they would see that she was meant to be a star. Mom and Grandma would be so proud. Maybe her father would even come to the play, and he would give her a huge bouquet of flowers. Sarah just knew that she was going to be famous!

Chapter 4: Smart Person

Mrs. Armstrong met with students individually once a week. She called it conferring. She never said it out loud, but since other teachers called it "conferencing," Sarah could tell that Mrs. Armstrong thought her term was proper and that the other teachers said it wrong. Sarah looked it up in Oxford Learner's Dictionary:

confer: *to discuss something with someone, in order to exchange opinions or get advice, -ing form* **conferring**.

When Mrs. Armstrong conferred with students it was cool. She let the student sit at the teacher's desk and she sat beside it. Sarah sat up straight and tall when she sat at the teacher's desk.

Today was Sarah's turn to confer with Mrs. Armstrong. She brought her reading journal and her science observation journal with her. Students could observe anything in the world that they wanted for the journal, as long as it wasn't people.

Mrs. Armstrong said that people didn't like to be observed and written about. It was rude.

First, they looked at the science observation journal together. Sarah's last few observation entries were about seed pods. They were so interesting and beautiful! There were poppy seed pods that looked like shakers with holes at the top in a flower design. Sarah had drawn sketches of them and wrote about shaking the poppy seeds out and licking them off the palm of her hand. They were just like the poppy seeds on a bagel! There were sweet gum seed pods that were big, gnarly and pokey. Sarah thought that it would be cool in a horror movie if they could come to life and fly around trying to poke people. There were also mimosa seed pods that reminded Sarah of lima beans spaced apart in a long, flat pod.

Mrs. Armstrong's eyes opened wide and she flipped through the journal to see all of the seed pod sketches. Then she smiled in a way that gave Sarah goose bumps.

"Sarah, these are exquisite! They could be framed as art! Did you know that sketches could be considered finished art?"

"Really? Thank you Mrs. Armstrong."

Despite the goose bumps, Sarah thought Mrs. Armstrong was just being nice, in the way that parents and teachers say stuff to encourage little kids, like asking what the scribbled picture was and then saying it was great even though they couldn't tell what it was in the first place.

Then they opened Sarah's reading journal. These entries were her free choice independent reading of The Twenty-One Balloons. First Mrs. Armstrong asked what made Sarah choose that book, and she seemed pleased that Sarah had made a goal of reading all the Newbery Award books. This one was pretty old. The first few chapters were really boring, but it got interesting when

Professor Sherman landed unexpectedly on Krakatoa, a volcanic island. The unusual inventions made by the people on the island were great, and there was an idea in the book that diamonds were only worth a lot of money because there weren't very many of them. The island in the story had a gazillion diamonds but the people there figured if they sold them all at once the price would go way down. So, sell a few for a lot of money or sell a bunch for just a little money. They only sold a few at a time. Sarah had written in her journal that it seemed weird to know that something was only worth a lot if it was hard to get. Mrs. Armstrong read the entries and nodded her head slowly. Then she looked at Sarah in a thoughtful way. She closed her eyes and seemed to be practicing what to say in her head before she spoke.

"Sarah, you are a very smart person. There are not many people your age that think about concepts like this."

Sarah heard what Mrs. Armstrong said, but she was mostly interested that Mrs. Armstrong kept using the words "person and people" instead of the words "girl, children, or students." She was thinking about the significance of these word choices when Mrs. Armstrong spoke again.

"Being smart is a good quality, Sarah. Be proud of your abilities. They don't make you better than other people, but I'm sure you've noticed that they make you a little different. Different is OK. Don't hide your abilities, but don't flaunt them. Others will resent you and think you are a snob just because you find easy what they find difficult. It's not fair, but it's true. Furthermore, smart people can accomplish a lot, but they still have to work hard. Sometimes smart kids find school work very easy, so they don't learn how to work hard or actually study. Then when they get to middle school or high school or college, they don't know how. I'm going to help you learn how to work and study, and it might seem unfair, but I expect a lot from you."

Sarah just said, "OK, Mrs. Armstrong" and went back to her desk.

Wow. Mrs. Armstrong thought Sarah was smart. She knew she was different, but she never thought it was because she was smarter than other kids. She knew she was different because she didn't have a dad, because she was on free lunch, because for some elusive reason she didn't fit in with the other kids. Now she was different because she was smart. Didn't sound so great. If school work was easy for her, why did Mrs. Armstrong want to make it harder? Why did she expect more from Sarah than anyone else? Why couldn't Sarah just be normal like the other kids? Maybe then she would be popular.

Sarah was hit again and again each day with the realization that Angela was not her friend anymore. Her stomach churned. She didn't have any friends. No one liked her.

Loneliness enveloped her. Grandma must have noticed Sarah's misery. She tried to cheer her up by pulling her into impromptu dance parties and treats of homemade lemonade. It didn't help, but Sarah understood that Grandma's love tried to absorb her unhappiness. Still, Sarah didn't tell her Grandma or her Mom about what had happened with Angela. She wanted to hide it away forever. Would they have called Angela's parents? Would they have told Tracy's parents? They depended on Tracy's parents for the basement apartment they rented. Would they believe that Sarah had taken Tracy's side just to protect their apartment? Would they have understood that it was really about telling the truth and doing the right thing?

Chapter 5: Learning Lines

In acting class everyone had to relax their bodies. That meant if the teacher, Mrs. Abousie, came up behind you, she should be able to gently tilt your head without warning, with no resistance. Lots of little heads lolled about, ready to be tilted. At the same time, they had to practice good posture. They had to breathe from their diaphragms, too, so that their voices would fill the theater. It was a real theater with red velvet seats and big lights aimed down at the stage.

Sarah enjoyed the improvisation exercises. Mrs. Abousie would tell a few of them their roles and relationships, and a starting event. Then the actors got to say whatever they wanted and act however they wanted. Mostly Sarah liked to act wicked, or tragically heartbroken. She could cackle like the wicked witch of the west or weep like Elsa from Frozen. Of course, the situations were different, but Sarah usually found a way to work in some evil laughs or tearful wails. It was *improv* after all.

Some of the other lessons were pantomime, which was pretty hard, and mirror, which could get silly. Once Sarah was paired with Michael for mirror. He was one of the best actors in the class, and one of only two boys. He was the mirror to Sarah. He mirrored her movements perfectly. She pretended to spray and wipe down a counter. Then she pretended to follow a butterfly. She began to move faster, and he kept up. Then she made up a goofy dance and laughed when she saw him doing the same exact dance. He didn't laugh out loud, but his face looked like he was laughing, just like hers.

When Mrs. Abousie called "Time," Michael bowed to Sarah. It made her feel all flustery, but nice.

By early October Mrs. Abousie said the class was ready for skits. Sarah got the part of an old lady who got lost walking home from the market. Angela got the part of the old lady's husband that went out searching for his wife and got lost, too. Michael got the part of the friendly neighbor that helped the old couple find each other and get home. Other kids in the class were assigned to different skits. They took their short scripts home with instructions to practice every day and learn their lines by next week.

Sarah planned to practice every day, but every time she meant to start there was something else that really drew her. On Sunday Grandma took her to the traveling carnival at the park. They shared a cotton candy and Sarah got to ride the Ferris wheel and jump for two sessions in the bouncy house. After their walk home it was dinner time and then shower and bedtime. No time to learn her lines for the skit. On Monday Sarah worked on the character mobile for her Holes book report. She bungled making holes in the figures. She had planned to put string through the holes and attach them to a hanger. But the holes were too big! The characters had big stupid holes in their heads! That was not what the book was about! She had to start all over, drawing the figures again. It took forever! But when she finally got done it looked pretty good. She taped a paper clip to the back of each character and used that to hold the string. No holes in her Holes characters! And, no time to learn her lines for the skit. On Tuesday Sarah decided that she deserved to relax and spend the evening vegging out with tv and chips. Mom joined her and they snuggled on the couch together. Mom stroked Sarah's hair and massaged her feet. It was so cozy. Sarah didn't work on memorizing her lines for the skit that night either. Wednesday should have been the day to buckle down and learn her lines, but Sarah concentrated on her reading and writing homework for a long time - longer than 40 minutes. Mrs. Armstrong wrote such encouraging comments in Sarah's reading/response journal that she really worked to make every entry meaningful. Comments like "True insight!" and "Interesting perception!" sent Sarah's spirits soaring. Again, she was too busy to learn her lines for the skit. By Thursday Sarah started to worry that she wouldn't be able to learn her lines for the skit. She read the script several times, but each time she got to the end Sarah realized that she had been thinking of something else entirely. It was like her brain was doing one thing while her eyes were doing another. She didn't recall a single line.

On Friday Sarah knew she couldn't learn her lines in time for the skit performance. It was a stupid skit anyway. The whole day was awful. First Sarah missed the bus and had to ask Tracy's mom to drive her. She would probably tell Sarah's mom or grandma, and then Sarah would get punished. Probably no tv all weekend. At school, Sarah couldn't find her homework in her backpack. The class always checked their own homework and made corrections, so while Mrs. Armstrong was walking around the classroom she stopped at Sarah's desk.

"Where is your homework Sarah?"

"I did it, Mrs. Armstrong. I guess I just forgot to put it in my backpack."

"If you don't have your homework ready to check in class, it's as bad as not doing it at all."

Sarah's face started to burn and she could feel her mouth turning into an ugly, downturned gash. Mrs. Armstrong walked away, and Sarah felt like she was sinking into a dark miasma. Her head hurt like it was being squeezed. This was the worst day of her life!

Sarah planned to sit alone at lunch and go to "solitude time" in Dr. Brennan's office at recess. She wouldn't have to talk to anyone. Dr. Brennan had board games, puppets, cozy corners where a kid could curl up in a soft blanket, and abstract artwork that invited one to imagine weird ideas. Anyone could drop in during recess time. It was a place that made Sarah feel safe at school. Safe from others, safe from feelings that were too scary to face, safe from time, safe from change and uncertainty.

At lunch, Ilaria sat next to her at the cafeteria table. Sarah looked away. She didn't want Ilaria to see into her eyes. Well, they didn't have to talk. There were too many feelings that Ilaria probably didn't know the words for in English. Neither of them spoke. But when it was time to clean up and go to recess, Ilaria slid a red Jolly Rancher on the table toward Sarah. Then she left. Sarah unwrapped the candy and indulged in the comfort of sucking on it as she walked to the psychologist's office.

The afternoon wasn't as terrible as the morning, but Sarah couldn't stop thinking about the disastrous skit performance ahead of her tomorrow, and wondering if her mom would be really mad about her missing the bus, and Mrs. Armstrong maybe not liking her anymore because she was irresponsible.

That night she tried again to read the script and learn her lines, but it was useless. All she could think about was how Angela and Michael would look at her during the skit when she couldn't remember her lines. Angela would be haughty and Michael would be disappointed, or worse - indignant.

It happened just as she imagined. Sarah could only remember her first few lines. When she missed her first cue Michael prompted her in a whisper. At the next cue Sarah just looked down and wrung her hands. Michael sighed and Mrs. Abousie called out the line loudly. No subtlety. No compassion. For the remainder of the skit it was Angela and Michael acting, Sarah standing immobile on the stage, and Mrs. Abousie saying Sarah's lines. Sarah left the theater afterward and waited outside for her mom to pick her up. She didn't want to see the other skits or face Angela and Michael.

At home, Sarah went to her bedroom and lay down. Everything was ruined - acting class, fourth grade, her whole life! She cried and cried, mushing her face into the pillow so her mom and grandma wouldn't hear. Then she slept.

Chapter 6: Ilaria

At recess, Ilaria played on the swings. She pumped her legs hard and leaned back to get more momentum. She went really high. The sun shone on her grinning face. She didn't stop until the whistle blew for lining up. Sarah had spent recess making lines in the dirt with the toe of her shoe. She didn't even kick the soccer ball away when it rolled under the bench where she sat. Angela and her friends practiced handstands and backbends, spotting each other and giggling when they fell.

When the kids lined up to go back to class, Sarah was right behind Angela, and Ilaria was right behind Sarah. Suddenly, Angela took a big step back, bumping hard into Sarah, who stumbled into Ilaria, who fell on the asphalt.

"Oh, SORRY!" said Angela, but it was the kind of sorry that meant she wasn't. You know, that sing-song way of saying "sorry." Sarah remembered times when

Angela had done stuff like that before to other kids. Now she was ashamed that she had just stood by.

Sarah glared at Angela and turned back to see that Ilaria was still down and crying quietly. Her right elbow was bleeding. The aide came over and told Sarah to take Ilaria to the nurse. Ilaria looked scared, so Sarah held her left hand and guided her down the hall. Nurse Ciacco washed Ilaria's elbow and put on a bandage with ointment. "Good as new!" she said.

Sarah didn't tell on Angela. Not this time.

Mrs. Armstrong re-organized the classroom that afternoon. She put Sarah next to Ilaria and she put Angela between two boys. Serves her right, thought Sarah.

Then Mrs. Armstrong announced that they were going to pair up for science fair projects. Sarah and Ilaria got paired, and Angela got paired with a boy, Ivan. The projects had to include a hypothesis, an experiment to test the hypothesis, data on a chart, and a conclusion. Pictures were optional. Real experiments - no volcanoes! They would have time to work on their projects in class, but could also meet outside of school to work on them. They had the last half hour of class to make plans with their partners.

Oh boy, how were Sarah and Ilaria going to make a plan when they didn't even speak the same language! Mrs. Armstrong approached the girls and told them that the ESL teacher had offered to help them figure things out during English as a Second Language (ESL) class. Whew! That wouldn't start until tomorrow, but Sarah got an idea about how to begin. First of all, she really wanted to do a plant experiment. She already knew a lot about plants. She drew a picture of a rose with a stem and leaves and thorns. (Rose blossoms were really fun to draw - it was like parenthesis marks curving around in a circle, layer after layer, each layer behind the spaces of the layer before.) Sarah pointed to each part of the plant and said what it was. After each part, she looked at Ilaria and said, "You say it." It took a few tries but then Ilaria got the idea. Flower, stem, leaf, thorn. Sarah mixed up the order of the parts she pointed to, just to be sure that Ilaria really matched up the pictures and the words. They said the parts again and again, until Ilaria was able to do it by herself.

The next thing Sarah taught Ilaria was how to do a high five. Yay!

Sarah sang "High Hopes" in her head on the bus and at the top of her lungs when she got home. Grandma smiled and tried to join in, but she kept mixing up the words and they both laughed so hard that Sarah's sides ached.

The ESL teacher, Ms. Blanco, always came to their classroom to pick up Ilaria. She'd peek in the doorway and give a little wave to Mrs. Armstrong, then shush the other ESL kids that she'd already retrieved from their regular classrooms. This time Sarah went with Ilaria. She'd never spoken to Ms. Blanco, but Ilaria always seemed happy to see her, so she must be nice. As they walked down the hall, the kids recited the names of the teachers in the classrooms they passed. The ESL room reminded Sarah of Kindergarten. There was a calendar, a number chart, a line of alphabet letters, and pictures with labels all over the walls. There was even a play kitchen with play food! There were dolls with all kinds of clothes, and a puppet theater with puppets - some were regular kid and grown up puppets, but the others were police, doctors, and firefighters. Fun!

Ms. Blanco got everyone except Ilaria and Sarah set up for a Smart table game that had them competing to match pictures with written and recorded words. Then she sat down to help Ilaria and Sarah with the science project. Sarah explained that she wanted to do a plant experiment, but she had no idea what. Ms. Blanco asked her a bunch of questions about plants, like all the things that they needed to grow. She asked if Sarah had a hypothesis or an idea for the experiment. She didn't. Then Ms. Blanco turned to Ilaria and began speaking in Spanish. Whoa! Were they talking fast or did it just sound that way because Sarah didn't understand the words?

Sarah began to fade out since she didn't feel like part of the conversation. She wondered if that was how Ilaria felt during regular class. She began to imagine living in a place where no one understood you and you understood no one. It must feel like you were alone, surrounded by people. Maybe it felt like they didn't see you.

Ms. Blanco turned to Sarah and said that Ilaria had an idea for the experiment. She wanted to know if plants would grow with filtered seawater. They could water different types of plants with fresh water and filtered seawater and see how they grew. She got the idea about filtering salt out of water by observing how her brother's t-shirts got white, salty edges around their sweat stains.

Wow! Sarah was impressed! Ms. Blanco helped them write out their hypothesis - *Plants grown with filtered seawater will grow as well as plants grown with fresh water.* They spent the rest of the ESL class time figuring out their experiment method and made a playdate plan to get started. Sarah would go to Ilaria's on Sunday afternoon. Turned out that she lived in a basement apartment right around the corner from Sarah!

Sarah told her mom and grandma about going to ESL class and the plan for the science project. They seemed perplexed by the partnership with a kid who didn't speak English, but no problem. They were pleased that Sarah was excited. Grandma agreed to go to the nursery with Sarah and Ilaria to buy plants for the project.

Neither Sarah or Grandma were prepared for the greeting at Ilaria's house on Sunday. When the door opened, there was a crowd of noisy people rushing to say hello at the doorway. Hugs and exclamations wrapped them in a crush. It was all in Spanish, so Sarah just smiled in response. After a few minutes the voices calmed, but the smiles held steady. Sarah had never felt so warmly welcomed. Ilaria introduced her mother - Josani, her two older brothers - Junot and Manny, and her grandparents - Jossiel and Luis. They each said hello. Sarah could tell that they had rehearsed the introductions. Ilaria's phrasing was formal and one by one they extended their hands for an awkward handshake. The hugs had been more natural.

Grandma pointed out different plants in the neighbor's gardens as she walked Sarah and Ilaria to the nursery. It was fall, so most of the flowers were marigolds/chrysanthemums, sedum, delphiniums, and geraniums. There was one Rose of Sharon that stopped them for a few moments of admiration, and a breathtaking bed of Sarah's favorite, pansies.

At the nursery the girls walked up and down the aisles, each holding up a plant and looking to the other for approval. Thumbs up meant they agreed. They settled on two geraniums, two marigolds, and two ferns. They would water one of each with filtered water from Long Island Sound and the others with tap water. Back at Ilaria's they got old t-shirts to use as filters. They made labels for the plants with masking tape. Ilaria's brothers went down port to scoop cans of water from the sound. Ilaria and Sarah filtered the seawater through the t-shirts. The experiment began!

Over the next few weeks Sarah and Ilaria met every Sunday to work on the experiment. Ilaria kept the plants on a south facing windowsill at her apartment. They shaded the ferns with some colored tissue paper taped to one corner of the window. It looked like stained glass. Ilaria watered their plants on Wednesdays, and Sarah watered them on Sundays. Junot wouldn't let them use his phone to take photos of the plants, but he took the pictures and printed them (with dates right on the photos!) at the high school. One of the girls measured the plants' heights with a ruler and the other one recorded the data on their chart. They took turns. Even more than the experiment, Sarah enjoyed hanging out with Ilaria and her family. The greetings were always effusive. Josani made delicious tostones snacks. Manny played a range of music on his guitar, from The Beatles to Aventura. The girls danced around to the music. Ilaria's brothers smiled at their little sister and spoke to her in gentle, amused tones. They knew more English than she did, but they spoke to her mostly in Spanish. Jossiel and Luis played cards at the table. The apartment was larger than Sarah's, but their family filled it to the brim.

From playdates for the experiment at Ilaria's apartment and going to ESL class, Sarah began to understand and speak a little (un poquito) Spanish. It was fun to roll r's and show off to the other kids in school by saying phrases like "Dónde está su libro?" (Where is your book?) and "Vamos a jugar un juego." (Let's play a game.) It was like having a secret. Everyone wondered what they were saying.

Ilaria began to raise her hand in class, especially in math because she knew how to say all the numbers in English now. Since they sat next to each other, Sarah was able to help her with reading, spelling, and pronunciation. It made her feel good to see Ilaria doing well in school and to hear that whispered "Thank you" from her.

Chapter 7: Acting is Work

Breathing properly, projecting her voice, and being expressive were not hard work, but learning lines for acting class was really arduous. Sarah could memorize the multiplication tables and spelling words by repeating them over and over, usually with Grandma or Ilaria. But memorizing lines for a skit or play was a lot more. Actors had to memorize the whole script. They had to respond to the other actors' lines with expressions and movement, and to recognize the cues that prompted their own lines. They also had to remember exactly where to move, and how and when.

Sarah wished they could just do improvisation. No matter how many times she read the scripts for her skits, her mind wandered. She could maintain the general momentum of the story, but the specifics sometimes got lost. She missed cues and flubbed lines. Mrs. Abousie was not pleased.

Michael tried to help her. He said remembering lines was like playing chess. (Not a game that Sarah knew how to play.) You just had to follow the prescribed plan. You just had to remember lines automatically and infuse them with expression. You had to be ready for the other actors to do their parts. Then you did your part. He would read scripts aloud with Sarah over the phone, but he became impatient once they put their scripts aside and she couldn't recall the lines. He didn't understand why it was difficult for her to remember every line in the proper sequence. Sometimes he yelled at her and once he hung up on her. It wasn't fun. Sarah didn't like rehearsing anymore.

She just wanted to wow everyone with her beauty and natural star qualities. She wanted to be "discovered"! How long did that take? Where were the talent scouts?

Sarah knew how proud her mom was that she could pay for theater school. It wasn't easy. She didn't earn much money, but she wanted to make Sarah happy and help her show off.

Sarah truly wanted to make her mom proud, but it wasn't looking good.

The next two skits were disastrous too, for Sarah. The other kids learned their lines pretty well. But they said Sarah ruined their skits because she didn't know her lines. For the next skit Sarah read the script every single night. But when she got on stage, she couldn't remember a single line and tried ad libbing. It didn't work. Her words didn't align with the script. The other kids in the skit just stopped and turned to where Mrs. Abousie always stood near the stage stairs. It was too dark beyond the stage to see her, but everyone knew she was there.

Mrs. Abousie called Sarah aside and said, "Sarah, if you don't learn your lines then you are letting the other students down. They deserve to have castmates that are prepared. I'm afraid that I'll have to drop you from the class if this continues. You have one more opportunity. If you don't learn your lines for the next skit, that's it."

"Yes, Mrs. Abousie. I really promise. I'll do it."

Sarah made the promise, but she didn't know how she was going to keep it. Learning lines was just too hard.

Chapter 8: Science Fair

All of Sarah and Ilaria's experiment plants had grown, some more than others, but the ones given fresh water had outgrown the ones with filtered seawater. Sarah and Ilaria wished that their hypothesis had been correct. But Mrs. Armstrong said that science experiments were about discovering facts, and that a disproved hypothesis discovered facts just as well as a proven hypothesis.

The next week the girls brought all of their handwritten materials to school so that they could type them and make the chart on a computer. Every team was allowed an hour every day in the computer lab to work on the project. Then the girls bought a three-sided display board at the school store. Sarah loved buying things at the school store. Besides regular school stuff, they sold silly character erasers, notebooks with artsy covers, backpack charms, and a bunch of other cool stuff. The fifth graders got to run it, and Sarah couldn't wait to stand behind the dutch door selling trinkets and supplies when she got to fifth grade.

When they were finished, their display board looked terrific. They put the hypothesis and a description of their method on the left side, the plant photos and growth chart in the center, and the conclusion on the right side along with a photo of Sarah and Ilaria together, their arms around each other's shoulders. In the photo they grinned, heads tilted together, and their eyes looked sideways toward each other. It was a picture of friends.

Excitement buzzed through the school on the day of the science fair. Classes were called down over the intercom to set up their displays on long cafeteria tables set up in the gym. Sarah's class had a substitute teacher for the day since Mrs. Armstrong had to supervise the science fair set up. When the sub brought their class to the gym, Mrs. Armstrong placed Sarah and Ilaria's project on the end of a table where everyone walking by would see it all by itself. It was a great spot! Mrs. Armstrong put one hand on each of their shoulders.

"I'm so proud of you two! Ms. Blanco told me how well you worked together planning your project, and now I see the beautiful display board you made together."

That evening, parents would come to see all of the experiments. That would be nice. For now, it was heartwarming that Mrs. Armstrong was proud of them. The sub had them walk by twos back to class, but she stayed at the head of the line so she didn't notice that Sarah and Ilaria were skipping at the end of the line. Not big skips, just short, low skips.

At twilight, Sarah walked to the school with Ilaria's family. It was so cold! But Sarah's mom had to work, so she couldn't drive them. Grandma couldn't walk that far in the cold. Sarah's eyes watered and her nose dripped. She pressed a knuckle of her gloved finger against each nostril and sniffed. Her fingers and toes felt numb. She linked arms with Ilaria. She squeezed her friend's arm to her side. Ilaria squeezed her arm back.

The gym was so warm from all the people in it that Mrs. Armstrong opened the doors to let some cold air in from outside. The crowd's voices melded into a low rumble. Sarah and Ilaria took turns standing by their own display and exploring the other projects. Some of the experiments were amazing! One team proved how oil spills in the ocean could be soaked up with human hair encased in nets. Another team had used different materials like cork, wool, and dirt to muffle sound, testing the effectiveness of each with an instrument that measured decibels. Sarah was excited to imagine how some of the experiments could change the world! Sarah and Ilaria's project wouldn't make headlines.

The other kids weren't that interested in their project. They just passed by and said "Hi." If the plants had been placed in front of the display board it might have caught their attention. Sarah would remember that for next year's science fair. The grown-ups that stopped to look at their project didn't ask questions or seem that interested. They said things like "Good work!" and "How cute!" Cute? What real scientist would want to prove something cute?

Mrs. Armstrong tapped on a microphone to get everyone's attention. She thanked all of the parents for coming and congratulated all of the students that participated in the science fair. Everybody would receive a participation ribbon, and the winners of first, second, and third place already had ribbons placed on their display boards. Everyone applauded as Mrs. Armstrong announced the winners. Really, Sarah thought, the projects that won truly did deserve it. They were great! Even so, she was perplexed by herself. Why wasn't she disappointed that her project with Ilaria didn't win?

She *was* disappointed that her mom and Grandma couldn't be there. But she was used to it. Mom had to work a lot and Grandma would have come if she could. That's just the way things were.

Chapter 9: Musical Revue

Just before the holiday break, Mrs. Abousie announced a new musical revue to be performed on the first Saturday in February. There would be voice and dance auditions in two weeks. Every student had to prepare a song or dance on their own or in groups. The choice was theirs. What an excited burst of squeals and exclamations erupted! Sarah watched as kids grabbed each other's arms, jumping about, sparkling eyes wide open. It was so exciting! Sarah stood by herself, waiting hopefully to see if anyone would invite her to share their excitement. No one came near. She was reluctant to approach any of the groups. What if they snubbed her? She realized that nobody had confidence in her. What if their excitement went flat and they just said OK because it would be mean if they didn't? She was too intimidated to try. She would have to audition alone.

When she got home Sarah hugged Grandma with a really fierce, long hug. Grandma hugged her back, letting Sarah decide when it was over. Then she said, "Tell me about acting class. Anything new?"

Sarah didn't look her grandma in the eyes. She just said, "Oh, we're going to have voice and dance auditions in a couple of weeks. I need to prepare a song."

She hadn't considered a dance number. A bunch of the kids took real dance classes. Sarah knew she couldn't compete with them.

"That's nice. Sounds like fun. Do you have a song in mind?" Grandma asked in her gentle, not too pushy voice.

"No," said Sarah. "I want to do something different. Something that the other kids don't already know. Something special."

All the way home in the back seat of her mom's car, Sarah had thought about what song to sing. Her voice was OK, not great. She didn't want to sing something that other kids might also choose or sing better than her. She had nothing, or as Ilaria would say, "nada."

"Hmm, maybe I can help. What about a duet with one of your friends in the acting class?"

"No, not a duet." Grandma would have been so sad if Sarah told her that she had no friends in acting class.

"OK, how about a song with whistling? Songs with whistling are happy songs! I know some great songs with whistling - Whistle While You Work / Don't Worry, Be Happy / I Whistle a Happy Tune / The Fishin' Hole."

Leave it to Grandma to know a gazillion songs and be ready to suggest them all, one by one, within every category you could think of. She was always humming a melody, sometimes repeating the same one over and over until Sarah's mom would cover her ears and say "Stop, please stop!" Grandma would look surprised and say she was sorry, she hadn't realized it was happening again. Grandma never used to be that musical. It was just in the last year or so that she had begun humming all of the time. And then, it seemed like every phrase she heard prompted her to burst into a song with that phrase in it. Like if someone said "The rain is gone," Grandma would sing "I can see clearly now the rain is gone..." Not just that line - the whole song! If someone said "Do you remember," Grandma would sing "Do you remember the days in September…" She knew so many songs! The whole thing was weird, and Sarah knew her mom worried that Grandma was losing it. Maybe Grandma's brain was sick. Maybe she was just getting old. Sarah didn't know.

"I don't know how to whistle Grandma."

"You don't? I'll teach you!"

And so it began. Grandma taught Sarah how to whistle, and she put The King and I on TV so Sarah learned the song I Whistle a Happy Tune. They sang it and whistled it, along with the movie, together, every night. The hardest part was trying to not smile so that she could whistle. You can't whistle while you smile! It was the best rehearsing ever!

When the day came to audition for the musical revue, Sarah felt confident. She gave the pianist the sheet music her grandma had borrowed. She stood center stage. She cleared her throat and closed her eyes, imagining her setting. She started singing low and soft, gradually building volume. She held the microphone close. Her voice wasn't warbly like Deborah Kerr's. Her voice was young and strong, pure and smooth. It was a kid's voice. The lyrics carried her into an imaginary world. Her whistling was clear. She held her head up high. She wasn't afraid. As the song ended, Sarah saw that her audience (everyone in her acting class) was standing, mesmerized. She had been so immersed in character and focused on her singing and whistling that the audience was invisible until this moment. Suddenly she was snapped into the here and now, aware of her surroundings. The audience began clapping and shouting "Sarah! Sarah!"

The public musical revue was a great success. All of the acts were good, and Sarah's performance of I Whistle a Happy Tune went very well. Her mom and grandma were there. Ilaria and her whole family were there. Tracy and her parents were there. (How did they even know about it?) Mrs. Armstrong and Principal Anesta were there. Everyone from theater school and their families gathered at the ice cream shoppe afterward. Michael stopped by Sarah's table with his parents and congratulated Sarah for a fabulous performance. Sarah blushed and murmured thank you. Angela was at a nearby table, but she pretended not to see Sarah. Sarah took it in, but it didn't hurt so much right now.

Later, as Sarah drifted into sleep, she wondered why being a star didn't feel as exhilarating as she had thought it would. It was nice. She was glad that people had enjoyed her performance. She was proud of her singing and whistling. She felt like Grandma had been behind her on stage, cheering her on. She visualized her mother's proud smile. They were with her, and that meant more than a million accolades from strangers whose faces she couldn't see in the audience.

Chapter 10: Advice

After the musical revue Sarah determined that she had to buckle down and really learn her lines for the skits and plays at theater school. Otherwise, Mrs. Abousie would tell Sarah's mom that she was kicked out. It was like Mrs. Armstrong said, Sarah needed to learn how to work at something that wasn't easy. She thought about how to learn her lines. Reading the whole script over and over hadn't worked. She should try some other way. Well, if two heads were better than one, maybe even more heads would be better. One by one, she asked for advice from Mrs. Armstrong, her grandma, and her mom.

Mrs. Armstrong suggested that she could break up the scripts into smaller parts. She should memorize the first small part and then repeat it as she added on the next small part, then repeat all of that as she added on the next small part, and so on. She would be building something big, adding on one small section at a time. Sarah tried it for her next skit, in which she played a boy that was bullied by his big sister. It worked! She memorized all of her lines and cues!

She tried the same strategy for learning her part as character Tom in the next play, The Prince and the Pauper. Again, she succeeded in remembering all of her lines and cues! It was fantastic! Well, actually she forgot one little line during the performance, but that was because Angela made a face at Sarah from off stage, distracting her.

Mrs. Abousie called Sarah over at the end of the class performance and said, "Sarah, you did a fine job with your part. I can see you've been working well to learn your lines. Keep it up and you'll be cast in better and better roles."

Sarah was so proud of herself! She had learned her lines! But it was interesting that Mrs. Abousie had said "working well," not "working hard." What, exactly, was the difference between working well and working hard? She'd have to think about that.

Grandma's advice was that she turn script lines into a song. "Songs are such an easy way to memorize, like the alphabet song when you were little!" she said. Well, that was true, but Sarah couldn't turn a whole play into a song. Perhaps it would work for some lines, like in a monologue. But the monologue would have to rhyme, wouldn't it? She would keep Grandma's idea in mind, but it didn't seem to be very helpful.

Sarah's mom suggested that she could add learning lines to her daily routines list. Sarah liked to make lists and check each item off as she completed it. She had turned Mrs. Armstrong's *Daily Routines* sheet into a weekly chart with a column for check marks and a row on the bottom to draw stars when everything for a day was checked. She *always* got a star, because she *always* completed every task. If it was on the list, it had to be done! Her mom had photocopied the chart on paper of all different colors, and Sarah taped a new one on her bedroom wall each Sunday. The old ones stayed up. The new ones expanded her record of accomplishment. It felt so good to see the mosaic of colored charts on her wall. Now she made a revised chart with a row for learning lines, but she called it *Rehearsing* (that sounded more professional) - *30 minutes a day.*

Sarah didn't ask Michael for advice. He had already shown how he gave advice.

Chapter 11: Winter

Darkness crept up the afternoon hours, saturating the neighborhood by the time Sarah's bus got to her block. When she opened their apartment door, Sarah could see Grandma standing downstairs at the little two burner stove. Hot chocolate aroma! Yum! It wasn't until she was blowing the tiny marshmallows across the surface of the chocolate that she noticed the new boots on the stairs. Sarah loved how her family kept one pair of shoes on the right side of each step. It looked like they were marching up the stairs all by themselves!

"Grandma! I got new boots!"

"It might snow soon. Can't have my girl's feet getting frozen."

Sarah could see that the boots weren't new. The blue coloring had faded a bit at the plastic toes. But she didn't care. They were pretty, with white fake fur peeking out from the tops. Grandma had probably bought them from the thrift shop at the church on the corner. She went to the church often, even when it wasn't Sunday. Sarah wrapped her arms around Grandma.

"You're the best Grandma ever."

It snowed on Sunday. Sarah wore her new boots outside to play in the snow. Tracy's parents were both shoveling snow from the sidewalk, and Tracy ran over to Sarah.

"I like your boots," she said.

"I like yours, too." Tracy's boots were green plastic on the foot part and thick green and blue plaid fabric on the ankle part. They didn't look fancy, but Sarah could tell they were expensive. Well, not really expensive, but kind of expensive.

Tracy stuck out her tongue. It took a second for Sarah to realize that she wasn't being mean. She was catching snowflakes on her tongue! Sarah did it, too. They both laughed and exclaimed that the snowflakes were delicious. This was the first time Sarah and Tracy had played together. They made a little snowkid from the pile of snow that had been scraped off the sidewalk onto the street and pushed by the snowplow to the bottom of the driveway. Tracy found a small broken branch that they used as an arm, positioning it so it looked like the snowkid was waving hello. Tracy had an old mitten that they put on the end of the branch. It looked great!

Sarah hoped that she and Tracy would play together again, not just in the yard. Trouble was, they didn't usually like the same kind of outside recess games. She wondered what indoor recess games Tracy liked. They would have indoor recess for a while, until all the snow melted and the ground soaked up the puddles it left behind. Too bad that most of the indoor recess games in the school were old and missing several pieces. Too bad *someone* didn't *buy* the school some new games. If there were new games, Tracy and Sarah could learn to play them together. Sarah wanted to make that happen. She *needed* to make

that happen. She began to make a
plan.

Chapter 12: The Big Plan

Sarah thought about the plan all the time. First thing when she woke up, last thing before she fell asleep, and running in the back of her mind throughout the day.

She didn't have money to buy games for the school. Her family didn't have money to buy games for the school. She didn't know anyone rich enough to buy games for the school. Maybe she could try to ask someone rich for the money, like that man in the next village who got rich with math in the stock market. Sarah didn't really understand how that worked, but she had heard Mom and Grandma talking about it over the newspaper one time. They said he was a *philanthropist.* Sarah had looked up the word. She couldn't remember the exact definition, but it meant a person that gives money and things to people just to be nice. She could write the philanthropist a letter. But when she asked Mom for an envelope, and what the man's name was, and how to find out his address, her idea got the kibosh.

"Why do you want to write to him?" asked Mom.

Sarah explained about the sorry state of indoor recess games at school, and Mom sat her down for a long talk. Long talks were OK, but Mom made them longer than necessary and repeated herself a lot. It was like she wanted to make sure Sarah's brain couldn't take off in a different direction. To be honest, when someone was talking Sarah's brain often took off in a different direction, whether it was Mom talking, or a teacher talking, or the tv talking. She would get an idea from something that was said and *zoom!* off went her brain. If only she could remember all the ideas her brain came up with, but by the time it settled down a few ideas had been lost along the way.

This time, Mom asked questions about the recess games and student council. She wanted to know who was the class rep for student council and when Sarah said it was Angela, Mom said, "Great! You're friends. You can ask her to make this a student council initiative."

Sarah lowered her eyes. Mom still didn't know about the rift in their friendship or Sarah's growing realization that Angela was a mean girl. Because she was always working, Mom hadn't noticed that Sarah and Angela didn't have playdates anymore.

"Sure, Mom. That's a good idea. I'll talk to Angela." Nope. Not ever.

Then Mom went on. "You know, the PTA should also be interested in recess games for the school. You know how they do all of that fundraising stuff? They use the money for student activities. I think recess games qualify! You could ask your teacher to inquire about making an in-person appeal to the PTA. It's always best to make requests like this in person. It's harder to say no to someone standing in front of you. But it would be better to have a group of students present a request for games to the PTA. That way it shows that this is important to several students."

Sarah decided to talk to some kids at recess. If she could get them interested, they could ask for Mrs. Armstrong's help to develop a presentation for the PTA. Sarah knew that PTA meetings were held every month, alternating between evening and afternoon meetings. Maybe the kids could make a presentation at the next afternoon meeting! *Of course* the other kids would want to be part of this! Why wouldn't they?

Chapter 13: Galvanizing Her Classmates

Over the next few days at recess, Sarah approached different groups of kids. They were playing the worn out games they always played, but once she started talking about her idea, one group after another said to quit bothering them and went back to their game. "Quit interrupting our recess," they said. "You're so annoying, Sarah," they said. She even got Mrs. Armstrong's permission to go to other classes to enlist them in her endeavor. Mrs. Armstrong said it would be a good exercise in developing leadership skills. But those kids were just as uninterested as Sarah's classmates. Why didn't they care? Didn't they want new recess games? Finally, Sarah confided her failure to Mrs. Armstrong.

"I'm glad we have this chance to talk, Sarah. I am impressed by your work on the enrichment assignments I give you. Also, I've noticed how much you help Ilaria while respecting her ability to do the work once she understands what is required. Your intelligence is enhanced by your humanity. I am honored to be your teacher and I hope we will be lifelong friends."

Friends? Could students and teachers be friends? It wasn't like they could have play dates. Maybe Mrs. Armstrong meant when Sarah was grown up. That must be it. Sarah felt proud that Mrs. Armstrong thought so highly of her.

Then Mrs. Armstrong told Sarah that she had to figure out how to *galvanize* the kids to take up her cause. She said Sarah should think about using feelings instead of just talking about her idea. She said Sarah should consider what makes people feel enthusiastic. So Sarah thought, and thought, and thought. She thought about what made her feel happy, or sad, or dreamy, or excited. She thought about the music in movies that could drive her to tremble with fear, send her heart racing with anticipation, or envelop her in weepy relief that everything was working out. She thought about the surge in her chest when she heard marching songs and watched parades. She thought about the outstretched arms and cries to heaven by preachers that her grandma liked to watch on tv. She thought about cheerleaders jumping around and shaking pom poms while they shouted cheers. The spectators cheered! She thought about how people feel when they see that other people are enthusiastic. They want to join in.

It seemed ridiculous that people didn't just consider ideas and decide if they agreed. They had to be drawn in by feelings. Seriously? Yet Sarah realized that she responded to the same influences. Mrs. Armstrong had a strong point. Sarah needed to galvanize the kids with feelings. Her plan needed music! Her plan needed cheers! Her plan needed volume and enthusiasm!

Later, Sarah sat on her bed with a composition book cradled

between her criss crossed legs and a pencil in her hand. She had the first few steps of the plan written down.

1. Ask Tracy to play an introductory Ta-da on her trumpet.
2. Write a cheer about recess games and enlist some kids to perform it with her.
3. Think of rhyming words to use in the cheer.

game / same

new / you / few / two / do

fun / done / one / none

recess / guess / success / yes

play / yay / say / day

OK. It shouldn't be too long. It should be quick to learn and easy to remember. It had to end with a short exclamation. Sarah wrote a cheer, then scribbled it out, then wrote another, then tore the page out and wadded it up, then wrote another. The last one wasn't too bad, but it wasn't great. She rewrote it with a few changes. Then she rewrote it again with more changes. There, that was good.

The next morning, before school, Sarah reread the final cheer. Nope, it wasn't final. She rewrote it again. Better. Every day, Sarah reread and rewrote the cheer. It kept getting better, but Sarah realized that it wouldn't be done until she could reread it and not decide to change anything. It took over a week, but she loved it at last.

Recess Games Cheer

Time for recess! *(Arms raised in triumph)*
Yes! Yes! Yes! *(Alternate arms pumping)*
We want to play! *(Twirl)*
But it's indoor recess every day!
(Thumbs down, stomping feet)
Our old games are broken down.
(Hands palms up, shoulders shrugged)
They're no fun. They make us frown.
(Arms akimbo, faces frowning)
We need *new* games! *(Jump and twirl)*
Not the same! *(Index fingers wagging no)*
New games, new games, not the
same! *(Jump and twirl)*
LET'S PLAY! YAY! *(Jump, jump, jump)*

That evening, Sarah knocked on the front door of Tracy's house. Tracy's mom answered. "Come in quickly Sarah. We don't want to let the cold air in!" Then she took Sarah to Tracy's room. Wow. What a cool room! There were posters of famous people with quotes taped to the walls - Eleanor Roosevelt, Ben Franklin,

Martin Luther King Jr., and somebody named Rachel Carson. There was a desk with a bookshelf above it. The top shelf had baseball trophies lined up. The lower shelves were stuffed with books. Sarah hadn't known that Tracy liked to read. Tracy's nightstand had a copy of The Twenty-One Balloons with a bookmark about halfway through. Tracy noticed Sarah's look of surprise at seeing that book.

"I saw you reading that and thought I'd give it a try. It's really good."

"Yeah, I like the inventions." Sarah said. Then she launched right into her plan to get new games for indoor recess, but Tracy's eyes glazed over with boredom. Time to switch tactics.

"I'd like to ask you for a favor. I wrote a cheer to get other kids interested, and I need a blast to get their attention. Your trumpet playing would be perfect! Could you play Ta-da on the trumpet right before our cheer?"

Tracy thought for a minute, then took her trumpet out of its case. Then she did it! She tooted Ta-da!

"That's perfect!" Sarah wanted to hug her, but she knew better.

"OK," said Tracy, "but don't try to get me involved in the cheer. Just the trumpet. That's all.

Sarah taught the cheer to Ilaria. Then they performed it for Sarah's Mom and Grandma. It was a hit! At school the next day they asked Mrs. Armstrong for permission to practice in the hallway during recess. Even better, she gave them permission to practice on the auditorium stage with an aide to watch over. Then she announced to the class that anyone who wanted to could go learn a cheer from Sarah and Ilaria during recess. Four girls and three boys raised their hands. It was going to be fabulous!

It didn't take long for the troupe (That's what Sarah called the cheer group.) to learn the cheer. They planned to perform it during recess the next day, but Mrs. Armstrong said it would be better to take the whole grade to watch in the auditorium. The troupe could perform on the stage just like they had practiced. The whole grade! Sarah quickly spread the word to the troupe. Was it just her, or was the buzz palpable?

The troupe and Tracy practiced on the stage one more time while the fourth grade classes made their way down to the auditorium. Sarah peeked between the stage drapes as the teachers got everyone to quiet down. Then the drapes opened. It was quiet for a moment, then Tracy stepped forward with her trumpet and played TA-DA! Tracy bowed. Everyone clapped and a few voices called out "Tracy! Tracy!"

Sarah counted to three, just loud enough for the troupe to hear. Then they performed the cheer. It was perfect! Some of the kids in the audience shouted "Encore! Encore!" so the troupe performed the cheer again. Sarah was so enthralled that she shouted, "Join in! Join in!" and they did! A few kids stood, then more and more. They had to spread out to do all of the moves. The whole grade stood and the troupe led them in the cheer. They did it three times! It wasn't until the classes were lined up and leaving the auditorium that Sarah saw Principal Anesta standing at the doorway and high-fiving with kids as they walked by. Mrs. Armstrong's class was last. Sarah looked into Principal Anesta's eyes and saw a sparkle. They fist bumped and fluttered their fingers outward like fireworks. They both laughed. Principal Anesta was cool.

The next few days seemed to fly by. The air was still cold, but the sun was bright and the mood at school was cheerful. Some kids repeated the new cheer during recess time. It was nice to hear. Kids seemed to smile at Sarah more and include her in their lunch table conversations. She felt calm and comfortable. The voice in her head was quieter. She didn't look around to see if others were noticing her.

Then there was Angela, who walked up to Sarah one morning and said, "You know, your cheer doesn't really rhyme. *Games* has an s at the end, so it doesn't rhyme with *same*. Just thought you should know."

Sarah's teeth clenched. She had considered that. She knew the s in games kind of messed up the rhyme, but it wouldn't work any other way. She had hoped no one would notice. It had to be Angela that noticed.

"You're just jealous, Angela!" There was nothing else to say.

Chapter 14: Playing Games

Angela's remark didn't matter anymore when new indoor recess games appeared the next week. There, stacked neatly on the classroom shelves, were boxes of new games - Apples to Apples Jr., Pictionary, Labyrinth, Qwirkle, Mousetrap, Checkers, Latice Hawai'i, and Table Hockey. A treasure trove of games!

Sarah was astonished! They didn't have to go to a PTA meeting or Student Council or anything! Who bought them? Now she could ask Tracy and Ilaria to play one of the new games with her. She knew Ilaria was her friend, and she believed that Tracy could become her friend too.

It turned out to be easy. Ilaria stayed close to her during most recesses, anyway. When Sarah asked Tracy to play one of the new games with them she said "Sure!" and grabbed the table hockey game before anyone else got it. She was quick! They took turns and got a little bit rowdy and loud. They were having so much fun!

That's when Angela and a few of the other girls surrounded them and began chanting, "Ilaria is hilarious! Ilaria is hilarious!" They mispronounced the name Ilaria so that it rhymed with hilarious, except for the s.

Ilaria froze. She may not have known the word hilarious, but she understood that Angela and the other girls were mocking her. Sarah put her arm around Ilaria's shoulders. Tracy jumped up. She got right into Angela's face and growled, "If you ever come near me and my friends again, I'll make you sorry." Her teeth were clenched and she shook her fist. Her face was deep red. Sarah was scared that Tracy would push or punch Angela. She didn't. She could have. But she didn't.

The aide that supervised them at recess came over then and said she'd have to let Principal Anesta know what had happened. Oh no!

Just when everything was going so well.

They all got called to the principal's office after recess. Principal Anesta asked each of them to tell the story of what happened.

Ilaria was crying so hard that she couldn't answer, except to say, "I'm sorry, lo siento, I'm sorry." (She didn't even do anything wrong.)

Sarah tried to be clear and factual, keeping the sequence straight. She tried to mimic Angela's taunt exactly.

Angela kept interrupting, exclaiming "Nuh uh! She's lying! I didn't!"

Tracy wouldn't say she was sorry.

The other girls muttered and their stories were a meandering mess.

Principal Anesta said she was disappointed that they couldn't all play nicely at recess. Then she said that Angela, her buddies, and Tracy wouldn't get to have recess for two days. Sarah and Ilaria weren't being punished, but they decided to sit out recess with Tracy.

Chapter 15: The Gift

It wasn't quite spring yet, but a few crocuses and daffodils promised longer days to spend outside. Sarah spent the early morning hours sketching blossoms with dew shimmering on their petals and leaves. Later in art class at school she painted, adding colors, highlights, and shading to the original sketches.

One afternoon Principal Anesta called on the intercom and said she wanted certain students to come to her office. Sarah was one of them. Were they in trouble? The three of them slowly slogged down the hallway, dreading whatever was about to happen. Principal Anesta stood smiling by her office door. Oh. Whatever it was, it must not be bad.

"Come with me," she said. "Mrs. Arthur has invited you to learn how to make mats for framing your artwork." Ohhhh!

They were the only kids invited to this special art class. Wow! That was cool.

Sarah's brain jumped ahead. She could make a mat for the painting she had done that day. It could be a special present for her grandma's birthday. Her mom wouldn't have to include Sarah's name on Grandma's card, because this would be a gift that was truly from her.

She really wanted to start right in cutting a mat for her grandma's birthday present, but Mrs. Arthur said they had to wait. "Let's just get on with it!" Sarah thought impatiently.

First, Mrs. Arthur showed them how to hold the mat cutter firmly and safely. Then she practiced with them, one at a time, hand over hand. Finally, she said they could cut on their own. But even then they didn't get to start on their final mats. Mrs. Arthur insisted that they practice on some scrap mats several times. Sarah was sure she could do it perfectly, but she didn't have a choice. Practice, practice, practice. Blah, blah, blah. So boring.

Sometimes the mat cutter slipped out of control, slicing sideways. Sometimes it snagged the mat and wouldn't move smoothly, making a rough edge. But after several tries the cuts became smoother and Sarah's hand grew more sure.

Finally, Mrs. Arthur stood beside Sarah and said, "OK! You are ready!"

Mrs. Arthur helped her measure and mark the guidelines. It felt so grown up to hold the mat cutter, carefully following the pale guidelines, pulling it toward her with just the right pressure. Then she held up the mat to examine her work. The angles were sharp and the edges were smooth! When her painting was mounted on the back of the mat, Sarah flipped it over and caught her breath, "Oh!"

Just like Mrs. Arthur had said, "Art can't be appreciated until it is properly presented."

The pale purple mat drew out the deeper colors of the crocuses, as if they were actually emerging from the snow, close enough to touch.

This would be the first, truly from her, birthday present. That evening, when Grandma unfolded the much reused and wrinkled tissue paper wrapped around the gift, her eyes misted over and she gulped until she blubbered.

Sarah hugged Grandma until the blubbering subsided, her eyes meeting Mom's gentle gaze. Family felt warm and squishy and good.

Grandma leaned the painting up against the wall on her nightstand. She said it would greet her every morning and evening, a happy hello and a peaceful goodnight.

Chapter 16: Sarah Confides in Tracy

The side yard was perfect for baseball practice. There weren't any windows and the next door neighbor's fence kept foul balls from straying too far. Of course, sometimes the ball bounced and hit the storm door to the apartment. Grandma would say "It gave me a start!" whenever that happened. Sarah thought it was hysterical when something gave her grandma a start - Grandma would rise up on her toes, her fingers would splay, and she would say "Uh oh" as her eyes opened wide. Then she would sigh and cross her hands over her heart.

Tracy and Sarah began throwing and catching the ball. Sarah found it surprising that she actually liked the way it felt to catch the ball in her mitt (a secondhand one from Tracy). She had never understood before why some kids liked sports, but there was a certain pleasure. The soft leather of the mitt absorbed the ball's impact, and the weight as it landed pulled gently at the muscles in her arm. Her body moved in concert with the ball, the atmosphere around her, and the ground below. Her body was in control of itself. Of course, she'd rather be twirling in a fancy skirt for "Star and Audience," which is what they played on Sarah's choice day. She would dance and twirl, becoming so dizzy that the world tilted and blurred. Then she would giggle, feeling euphoric. Her body was out of control! But today was Tracy's choice day and that meant playing catch. The deal was, alternate choice days - it was only fair.

"Hey Tracy, is your dad the coach for your baseball team?"

"No, he doesn't get home from work in time for practice on weekdays. It stinks, because the kid whose dad is the coach usually gets to be the starting pitcher. So I'll never get to be a starting pitcher."

"But he goes to your games, right?"

"Yeah, the games are on Saturdays, when he's off from work. You know, I've been wondering, does your dad live far away, or did he die or something? I've never seen him."

The ball passed back and forth a few times while Sarah worked up her courage. Tracy wouldn't understand. Her family was perfect.

"He never wanted to be a dad, so my mom told him to get out of her life."

That's what her mom had told her a long time ago, when Sarah asked why the other kids had a dad and she didn't. Grandma had tried to shush her mom with a grimace and waved her hand as if she were brushing something away. Even if their parents were divorced or never got married, the other kids knew their dads and got to see them on weekends or holidays. Sarah didn't even know who her father was. He never wanted to be a dad. He never wanted to be *her* dad.

Then her mom had said, "We don't need him anyway."

Afterward she had taken Sarah to the movies. Sarah could tell that her mom didn't want to talk about it, so she didn't bring it up again. She didn't want to upset her mom. But the shadow of a father she didn't know hung around her thoughts, always.

She wasn't going to tell Tracy about listening to Mom and Grandma the other night, when she was supposed to be asleep.

But then Tracy said, "I'm sorry Sarah. That must hurt your feelings so bad."

Sarah's face scrunched up and hot tears flooded from her eyes. She dropped the ball to the ground and ran to Tracy's porch step, where she sat sobbing. Tracy sat down next to her, just quietly being there.

When Sarah's sobs dwindled, she snorted up her runny nose and wiped tears from her face with her sleeve. She had to tell somebody what she had heard.

"I just found out that my father got married and adopted his wife's little boy. I guess he didn't want to be my dad because I'm a girl."

That was it. She had confided the worst thing in her life to Tracy. She glanced over at her new confidant, a little scared about trusting her with the secret.

"Please don't tell the other kids."

"Safe secret," whispered Tracy, "Safe secret."

Chapter 17: Batting Cage

One Sunday Tracy's dad took them to the batting cage. Sarah watched as Tracy took a batting stance and swung her bat at each ball the machine pitched to her. The balls came at regular intervals. Tracy swung over and over, hitting a lot of the balls but missing a lot too. Then the pitching machine stopped.

"Your turn Sarah," said Tracy's dad.

"Me?" Sarah was incredulous.

Tracy handed her the helmet and the bat. Sarah was sure she wouldn't be able to hit a ball even once. She went into the cage and tried to imitate the stance that Tracy had taken. Tracy's dad showed her how to choke up on the bat and told her to keep her eyes on the ball.

She tried, but when she saw the first ball hurtling toward her she bent down and twisted around. She closed her eyes and hoped the ball wouldn't hit her. Tracy's dad stopped the pitching machine and came into the cage.

"It's ok Sarah. The first pitch is scary. Don't worry. You'll get it. Can you try again?"

Sarah nodded. This time she held her position, but she swung the bat too high and too soon. Tracy's dad stopped the machine again and told her to practice swinging the bat horizontally. She did, and then she said "I'm ready."

Mostly she missed the balls, but she didn't cringe or close her eyes. When she did hit a ball, Tracy and her dad cheered and said "Good swing!" She was so proud.

Sarah hoped they would take her to the batting cage again.

That night, Mom and Grandma's conversation in the kitchenette spiked with laughter, making Sarah smile. It was comforting to hear them nearby, happy. The night air carried the sound of the ferry boat's horn as it left the harbor. From her open bedroom window, Sarah could see stars just beginning to sparkle against the violet evening sky.

Her upper arms and calves ached when she stretched, but in a way it felt good. She ran her fingers along the firm muscles that bulged just a little bit. She was tired. She was sleepy. She closed her eyes, listened to her own gentle, regular breaths, and dreamed …

Over the next few weeks, Tracy's dad played catch with them and took them to the batting cage a lot. He said that he wanted to get Tracy ready for the season. Sarah was so glad that they brought her along. She was getting better. Not as good as Tracy, but better.

In the back seat, Tracy and Sarah subtly elbowed each other just for fun on the way home from the batting cage. They were baseball buddies.

Chapter 18: Acting Success

Ever since she had learned how to memorize lines, acting class had become more enjoyable. Sarah learned her parts for the skits and plays they performed, and now she had the freedom to elaborate on the physical movements, facial expressions, and vocal intonations that rounded out her characters. She perfected a stage whisper for her evil character in a play about a cruel landlord. She lightly danced/skipped as a young girl in a skit about a charming child that captured everyone's hearts. She successfully managed to seem busy arranging flowers during a monologue by an angry character opposite her, all the while expressing private anguish with her eyes, mouth, and posture.

The other kids in the class were glad to be cast with her. Michael even said that he particularly enjoyed acting with her. Sarah enjoyed the repartee that she and Michael developed in an abridged scene from

Shakespeare's Taming of the Shrew. They were playful together. He said that they had good stage chemistry. Sarah hoped that they could be cast together for the best plays.

Of course Angela was also popular in acting class. She learned her lines well and showed talent. When they were cast together, Sarah and Angela played their parts. They were adept young actors, but there was an underlying tension between them and the pieces just didn't play well. Mrs. Abousie cast them together less and less often.

With every performance, Sarah's confidence as an actor grew. She was good! Mrs. Abousie complimented her and began to give her choice parts. Sarah regaled her mom and grandma with stories about theater school, sometimes acting out full scenes, playing all the parts. They watched, rapt by her performances, applauding enthusiastically at the end. They were proud of her. Mrs. Abousie was proud of her. She was proud of herself.

Chapter 19: Getting Older

Sarah knew something big was up when her mom told her to sit on the ottoman, grandma turned off the tv, and they sat facing her from the sofa.

"Am I in trouble?"

"No sweetheart, we just want to talk to you about this Saturday," said her mom. "I have to work."

This Saturday? This Saturday was audition day at theater school. If mom had to work she couldn't drive Sarah there. A whooshy kind of noise filled Sarah's head. She jumped up and blurted "But I have to go to the auditions or I won't get to be in the big play!"

"Calm down, Sarah," said her mom. "Grandma and I talked about it and we have made a decision. You are getting older now. We think it would be OK for you to ride your bike there. It's only a couple of miles. We know what a good bike rider you've become and we are counting on you to keep yourself safe."

Sarah sat down. The whooshy noise went silent. Wow! "Ok, Mom. I will keep myself safe. I won't talk to strangers. I'll ride on the right side of the street. I'll stop at the stop signs. I'll walk my bike across the intersections, just like you taught me. I promise."

Her mom smiled and her grandma patted her on the shoulder. Sarah felt so much older.

Chapter 20: Audition Day

Before her eyes opened, before the smell of Grandma's coffee wrinkled her nose, before she recognized the swish of the washer and the clank of metal buttons tumbling in the dryer on the floor above, the buzzing of the neighbors' lawn mowers and edgers reminded Sarah that today was Saturday. Not just any Saturday - *the* SATURDAY. Today was the biggest, most important day of her life. It was audition day at theater school.

Mrs. Abousie had given very clear instructions about audition day. Everyone had to be at the theater by 11:00, ready to read "cold" for all the parts. Which play they would be performing in June was a big secret, not to be announced until just before auditions began. It would be a fairy tale or children's story of course - that's what the theater school always did for the big play at the end of the season. But which one? It was so exciting to think of the possibilities!

Sarah ran to Grandma in the kitchenette and grabbed her hands, dancing and bouncing around until Grandma pulled her close and squeezed so tightly she couldn't move. Grandma called that the "swaddling hug." She always did that when Sarah was jumpy and it really did help her calm down. For the next couple of hours, until it was time to go, Grandma made breakfast and packed a lunch. She helped Sarah comb out her hair while it was still wet from the shower and pulled the sides up into a clip at her crown. (Sarah loved that part of her natural head was called a crown!) Then it was time to get dressed.

She wanted to wear one of her dressiest dresses. Sarah knew that she had to look glamorous if she wanted the starring role in the play. Stars don't look just regular. Grandma wouldn't understand how important that was, so she really didn't have to know.

Sarah put on her ruffled dress and her strappy sandals with kitten heels. Then she rolled up her white stretchy pants and pink camisole top and tucked them into her backpack, under the lunch bag, to wear home after auditions. She knocked on the bathroom door when she could hear Grandma running the shower.

"Bye Grandma, I'm going now," she called out.

"Wait, let me give you a kiss for luck!" Oh gross, Grandma stepped out of the bathroom wrapped in a towel. She had a big smile on her face until she looked down and saw what Sarah was wearing.

"Oh no, go put on your pants and sneakers. You can't ride your bike in those clothes."

Sarah put on her camisole, pants, and sneakers, and tucked the sandals into her backpack with her dress, being careful to put the soles facing down in the backpack. Then she rushed out the door without stopping for further inspection.

Outside, Sarah tapped on Tracy's bedroom window. She hadn't

really planned this, but Tracy would probably help her. After they talked for a minute, Tracy pulled Sarah's backpack in and said she could change there, but she would have to sneak back out through the window so that they didn't both get into trouble. Tracy had a baseball game that afternoon and she didn't want to get grounded and miss it. It was a little awkward for Sarah to climb out of the window in her dress and strappy sandals, but finally she was ready to go. She grabbed her backpack and rode off on her bike as fast as she could.

She was about halfway there when it happened. The road was a little bit downhill, but that wasn't the problem. There were a few cars driving past Sarah on her bicycle, but that wasn't the problem. The sun was glaring in Sarah's eyes, but that wasn't the problem. The problem started as a little tug at Sarah's waist. Then it felt like a pull. Then a bigger pull and Sarah felt herself tilting toward the pull. She looked down over her shoulder and realized that the hem of her dress was caught in the spokes. She tried to brake, but her right strappy sandal slipped off the pedal and then her foot turned toes down and the asphalt scraped so roughly that she cried out. Then she fell. She was on the ground by the curb. Little bits of rock and dirt were embedded in her bloody toes and knee, the heel of her hand, and her forearm. Her dress was wound up in the spokes of her back wheel. The straps on her right sandal were broken. She didn't look glamorous. She was a mess. Tears filled her eyes.

It took a while to untwist her dress from the spokes, and the fabric was torn at the waist. There were grease stains, too. The dress was ruined. The sandals were ruined. The scrapes stung. Sarah changed her shoes and draped the dragging part of the dress over her arm. She walked her bike the rest of the way to the theater. Luckily, she got there before most of the other kids and no one noticed her slipping into the bathroom. She washed her scrapes and changed her clothes, stuffing the dress and the sandals into the garbage and covering them with some paper towels. She didn't want anyone to know what had happened and she never wanted to think about those clothes again.

All of the theater students sat on the edge of the stage, facing their teacher, Mrs. Abousie. She held a stack of script booklets in her hands, waiting for all of the chatter to subside while she took deep breaths to prepare for "projecting her voice."

"Ladies and gentlemen, I am pleased to announce that this year we will be performing the play (she paused to build almost unbearable anticipation) *Alice in Wonderland, Jr.*"

Everyone applauded. Then auditions began. Partners were assigned a series of parts to read cold with each other while everyone watched. No talking allowed in the audience. Script booklets sat in a stack by the edge of the stage steps for the performers to pick up on their way to audition - no reading ahead. Sarah and Angela were assigned together but they had to wait quite a while for their turn. Why had Mrs. Abousie assigned them to audition together? Was it some kind of test? They didn't sit together, but while auditions were going on, Sarah glanced furtively at Angela.

Her blonde hair was pulled softly back, making her eyes look huge. Did she have on mascara or eyeliner? She wore a pretty blue dress. Sarah thought about her own brown hair and the casual clothes she had on. Which of them looked more like Alice, the star of the show?

When it was their turn, Sarah and Angela read for Alice and the Caterpillar, Tweedle Dum and Tweedle Dee, and Alice with the Mad Hatter. Mrs. Abousie assigned their characters and told them the pages to read from in the script. At least Angela wasn't given the role of Alice to audition.

"Whooo are youuu…?" Angela the Caterpillar said imperiously.

"I..I..I.. hardly know sir," stuttered Sarah as Alice. Good thing the stutter was actually part of the script. Sarah might have stuttered anyway, she was so nervous.

***

For Tweedle Dum and Tweedle Dee they had to read in unison, finishing with

"…but as it isn't, it ain't. THAT'S LOGIC!"

They actually did a pretty good job together, and both Sarah and Angela giggled at the end.

***

Sarah got to read for Alice again while Angela read for the Mad Hatter

"I don't think…"

"Then you shouldn't talk," Angela the Mad Hatter said quite matter of factly, with her mouth turned down and her left eyebrow raised (just one eyebrow!) while looking sideways at Sarah.

Wow, that was really good! Better acting than anyone so far.

Back in the audience, Sarah's thoughts meandered. No way was she going to get the part of Alice. Or maybe she would. She didn't look like Alice, but Angela did. Still, if she wished it hard enough, she might get the part. Laughing together in the audition had felt so friendly and nice, like when they were friends, not in the feud that had simmered through every day at school. But what if Sarah got some ugly part like one of the Tweedles or the Caterpillar? She was sure that Angela would tell everybody and they would probably call her those names every single recess!

Auditions were finally over.

"You were all wonderful!" exclaimed Mrs. Abousie. "The cast will be announced next week."

On the bike ride home, Sarah took a detour over to the baseball field where Tracy's game was being played. It wasn't far and Mom wouldn't be home from work yet anyway. When she got there it was the bottom of the seventh inning and Tracy was on deck. Tracy's folks waved to Sarah, so she put her bike at the rack nearby and sat with them on the bleachers. The sun was getting low and there was a cool breeze to soothe the scrapes that still stung a little. Auditions were over. Her ruffled purple dress and strappy sandals were gone. The most important day of her life hadn't been what she'd anticipated.

Tracy hit a fly ball way past the shortstop, into the outfield. She made it to second base and the kid on third base made it home safe. Throughout the rest of the game, Sarah imagined herself in the positions in play. Her clenched hands were jolted each time the bat connected with a pitched ball. Her shoulder slung forward as the ball was thrown, from the pitcher to the batter, and from the outfield to the infield. She cheered for each successful play by Tracy's team, the Downport Dolphins. All that practice with Tracy had taught her how the game felt.

Tracy's team lost the game, but it was close. One of the team parents bought vanilla ice cream with real sugar cones for the team from the truck at the curb. Tracy's parents bought an ice cream cone for Sarah. Everyone was laughing and smiling, most of them with ice cream smears around their mouths. Sarah laughed with them. She wondered if she looked as goofy as they did. She hoped so. Afterward, Tracy's mom offered to drive Sarah home. It was almost dusk, an unsafe time to ride a bike, and Sarah's bike could fit in the back of their SUV.

"I'm surprised that your mother lets you ride your bike alone, even during the day," said Tracy's mom when they were in the car.

Sarah didn't say anything. She knew that her mom would feel bad if she knew what Tracy's mom thought. It wasn't her mom's fault. She had to work.

Chapter 21: Sleepless

Sarah wanted to sleep, but her mind kept replaying the auditions. Were all the other kids wondering why she looked so bedraggled? Her knee had bled a little through the stretchy white pants. Her hair had come down from the clip on one side. She should have changed clothes when she got to the theater, not before riding her bike. Hopefully mom wouldn't notice that the dress and sandals were gone.

That eyebrow expression that Angela did was a pretty cool trick. Sarah got up and went to the bathroom mirror. Every time she tried to raise just one eyebrow, the other one went right along. She tried holding one eyebrow down with her fingers while raising the other eyebrow as high as she could. It didn't quite work, but if she kept at it, her forehead muscles might learn.

Was Angela truly better at acting? What if *she* got the part of Alice? Sarah didn't want any other part. No other part, only Alice. Not the Queen of Hearts, not the Rabbit, neither of the Tweedles, not the Cheshire cat, not the Caterpillar, not the Mad Hatter, not the Dormouse. No...other...part... only Alice.

Back in her bedroom, it was hot and stuffy. How was it possible for air to feel heavy? Sarah kicked off the sheet and threw the pillow on the floor. Then a mosquito bit her ankle and she slapped it, hard. A little blood smeared on her hand. Sarah got up and turned the fan on high. It didn't really cool the room, but the feel of air blowing chilled the sweat along her hairline and the whirring noise muffled the hooting and hollering of teenagers driving by in their rattletrap cars. Sarah wondered if those kids were really having fun or just showing off. Did they feel the way she did when she giggled a lot so that other people would notice her? It seemed fun when she was giggling, but the doubts came after. Did they like her? Did they think she was annoying? Did they whisper about her and make fun?

Sarah hummed into the fan, letting the melody carry her away. It was a childish game with the fan, making her voice vibrate. Then she opened her mouth wide, pushing a range of notes far out of herself. It was music, it was a scream, it was a relief.

Mom opened the bedroom door. "Sarah! Be quiet and go to sleep!"

Chapter 22: Tracy Gets Hurt

All week, Sarah wished for the time to pass quickly so that she would finally know what part she got in the play. All week, Sarah tried to reassure herself that she, not Angela, would be cast as Alice. (She didn't even consider the possibility that neither of them would get the starring role.) Angela hadn't spoken to Sarah since the auditions. She was probably still mad about what happened with Tracy back in September. She was probably still mad about what happened with Ilaria, not so hilarious after all. The giggles they shared during the Tweedle Dum and Tweedle Dee reading probably didn't mean anything to Angela. Sarah wished she didn't care either. She still missed their fun together.

Tracy was absent from school on Thursday, so Sarah brought the homework sheets to her after school. Tracy's mom opened the door.

"Hi Sarah. Thanks for coming by. Tracy is in her room. She's not sick, but she hurt her arm." Tracy's mom didn't really look at Sarah or smile like usual. She must be worried.

Tracy's right arm was in a sling. She said that last night she was practicing pitching with her dad when her arm suddenly started to hurt. By this morning she couldn't move her arm, so that's when her folks took her to the emergency room to get an x-ray. Her parents, and even the doctors, said you couldn't break an arm just throwing a ball, but the x-ray showed that Tracy's humerus bone *was* broken and there was a huge cyst *inside the bone!* The doctors had said they couldn't do blood tests to see what caused the cyst until the broken bone had mended. Tracy's mom and dad kept glancing at each other while she told Sarah about her injury.

Tracy couldn't even write her homework, so Sarah stayed and they did their homework together. They would decide on the answers together and Sarah would write it for both of them. It was fun, especially when they had different answers and did what

Mrs. Armstrong called "defending their points of view."

Tracy was going to the orthopedic doctor the next day for a cast. It would be on for 6 - 8 weeks! Sarah hung out with her for a while, but every time Tracy moved she moaned and grimaced. Poor Tracy! Sarah began stuffing their homework folders into her backpack, getting ready to go home.

"Sarah, I have a big favor to ask you. My dad says I'll be off the team for the rest of the season. Would you take my place? I mean, not pitch for the team, but play on the team? We have to have at least nine players, and if I don't play we only have eight. I think the coach would say it's OK, and you're getting really good at catching and throwing, and even batting. If you were playing, my dad could drive us and I could be there to watch. You're my best friend, and I'd really like it."

Sarah's thoughts boomeranged around inside her head. Tracy was her friend. She said Sarah was her *best friend.* Sarah, on a baseball team? She liked having a catch and practicing at the batting cage down port with Tracy, but she had never imagined really playing on a baseball team! What if Tracy and her dad were just being nice? What if she wasn't really good enough to be on the team? Wait! If she was on the baseball team, she couldn't be in the play. But what if she had actually won the role of Alice after all? If she chose baseball she would never know. If she chose the play, she would let Tracy down. Baseball games were on Saturdays, the same as theater school. She couldn't do both. She could only choose one.

Tracy was silent, apparently waiting for an answer *now.*

Sarah took a deep breath. "Yes. I'll play on your team. Yes! I will! I'll do my best! You can count on me!"

Suddenly all of the anxiety swirling around Sarah washed away. She let go of her worries about being cast in the play. The grasp of her lost friendship with Angela was released. She didn't need to be a star right now. She needed to be a friend. She smiled. Tracy smiled. They nodded to each other.

Chapter 23: Downport Dolphins vs. Play It Again Penguins

Coach Joe touched Sarah's shoulder and said, "I need you to take left field."

Sarah's stomach felt tight and queasy. Everything beyond the next step toward the outfield seemed glaringly bright. It was really happening. She was going to play baseball in Tracy's place. Well, not exactly Tracy's place, because Tracy pitched or played shortstop, but still, Sarah was playing because Tracy couldn't. What if she messed up? Would Tracy be disappointed? What if they lost the game because of her? Would everyone on the team blame her?

As Sarah took her place in the outfield, she put on her mitt and held the brim of her cap low to shade her eyes so she could see Tracy on the bleacher. Tracy gave a high thumbs up with her good arm, making Sarah grin. Sarah took a deep breath, sinking into a calm that felt just right. The mitt was soft on her palm. The pitcher, Tommy, stood on the mound and turned to look at each of the players on the field. It was like he was saying "I'm counting on you." Then the Penguin's batter walked to the plate. OK, the inning was about to start.

No hits made it to left field. It was kind of boring to be in the outfield, but Sarah knew she had to be ready if a ball did fly out to the whole big area that spread behind second and third base. She watched the game and stayed ready to run, but the first half of the inning ended without her getting to do anything but stand there. No runs. The Penguins hadn't scored. The Dolphins walked in. One of the parents handed out water bottles and Coach Joe announced the batting order. Sarah was number eight.

The first Dolphin's batter hit a foul ball and then was out with a pop-up fly. The second batter made it to first base. The third batter's hit flew past the pitcher and the shortstop, then bounced and rolled toward the left outfielder. She picked it up and threw it to second base. Wow! What a throw! The second baseman caught the ball and tagged the hitter, then threw the ball to home plate for an out on the runner. Oh no! The Dolphins hadn't scored a single run in the first inning.

Back in the outfield again, Sarah watched the game intently. Two outs, two runs. The next batter hit the ball on the first pitch. It looked like it might fly out to left field. Sarah's heart pounded as she watched the ball and ran to where it seemed to be heading, but the shortstop ran backward, jumped high, and caught it. Sarah and the shortstop had almost run into each other! Oh boy, close call.

Back at the dugout, the Dolphins gave each batter a "Keep your eye on the ball," "You can do it!" and other encouraging remarks. That's nice, thought Sarah, and she joined in. Three batters were up before Sarah. The first two made hits and got to base, and the third one got out at second base but managed to get the other two runners into home base. Two RBIs! Sarah had practiced in the batting cage while she was on deck. She could see Tracy and her dad. She remembered all the coaching they had given her and tried her best. Sarah was up. The Penguins changed pitchers, and he practiced throwing to the catcher several times before Sarah went to the plate. Her hands were sweaty, so she wiped them on her thighs. Then she picked up the bat and held it high over her shoulder. She faced the pitcher. The first pitch was a ball, and she held her bat steady. The second pitch looked good, and Sarah swung hard, but too soon. She missed the ball. Strike one! Her teammates called out, "C'mon Sarah, you can hit!" The next pitch was a little high, but Sarah swung anyway. She hit the ball and it fouled out. Strike two! The next pitch was good, and Sarah loved the sound when her bat connected with the ball.

It was a solid, ringing ping! The ball was headed straight to the pitcher, but low. It might hit the ground before he could catch it. Sarah dropped the bat and ran toward first base. "I hit it! I hit it!" she thought. As much as she wanted to turn and look at where the ball was, she kept her eyes forward. The first baseman was looking toward the pitcher's mound with his hands at chest height, ready to catch a throw. Sarah wished she could slide into first base, but she was scared and really didn't know how to do it. She just ran as fast as she could. Then she saw it. The baseman caught the ball and turned to her. His foot was on the base. She was out. Sarah walked back to the dugout. She wasn't upset. Actually she felt proud that she had made a good hit and the run was exhilarating! Her teammates patted her on the back and said things like "Good try" and "Next time." Sarah smiled. The next batter hit the ball toward third base. The third baseman was able to get the ball and throw it to the first baseman before the batter got there. The inning was over. The game was tied.

As the sun rose higher and the game went on, Sarah felt rosy and mildly pleased. Even though no balls made it to her in the outfield, even though she didn't get to bat again, even though she wasn't a star baseball player, even though she wasn't very good, she was part of a team. She had teammates. She belonged. The Penguins won, the Dolphins lost. Still, it was a good game. There were a lot of good plays on both sides. After the game, the Dolphins (including Tracy and her dad) met up at the ice cream shoppe for a post-game treat. High fives all around, and declarations that next time they would win. It was a good day.

Chapter 24: End of Fourth Grade

The last writing assignment of the year was a letter to the students' future selves. It was to be a personal memoir about fourth grade. Mrs. Armstrong said she would mail them to the kids when they graduated from high school. Really? What did she have, boxes of old kids' letters that she mailed out every year? Bizarre.

Dear Me (Sarah),

Fourth grade was not how I thought it would be. When the year started I was just a little kid, but now I'm almost ten - double digits! A lot happened this year, some good, some not so good.

My best friend isn't Angela any more, but that's good because she turned into a mean girl. Actually, she was always mean. I just didn't realize it before. Now I have two best friends, Tracy and Ilaria. They are both nice.

I found out that even a girly girl like me can like pants and baseball. Who knew?

Angela and her new best friends say mean things about Tracy and me, like that we are in love with each other. We're just kids! We're not in love with anybody yet! She also makes fun of Ilaria's accent. Mom says ignore her. Grandma says Angela's feelings are hurt that we aren't friends anymore. Maybe I would be friends with her again if she stopped being mean. Maybe when I get this letter in the mail (in almost forever from now) we'll be friends again.

Anyway, Tracy is a good friend, even if she is a little bossy about teaching me baseball. I'm a little bossy about teaching my other best friend Ilaria about how to speak English. Sometimes I make her say English phrases a gazillion times until they sound right. But I don't make fun of her.

In the grades before this I never really got to know the ESL kids, but Mrs. Armstrong gave me the classroom job of helping Ilaria for the whole year. She said it was a really important *diplomatic* job, connecting cultures. I even went to ESL class with Ilaria sometimes. Then I got invited to neighborhood parties with her and we dressed up and danced. Seems like the Dominican Republic families are always laughing and kissing each others' cheeks, and talking with exclamation points. It is so fun!

The worst thing this year is that I wasn't in my theater school's big production of Alice in Wonderland, Jr.. Angela got to be Alice, of course. Mom was pretty mad that I quit acting class to play baseball. I probably should have talked to her about it first. Grandma said I didn't really want to be an actress. She said that people show what they really care about by the choices they make and the way that they actually spend their time.

I still wish I could be a famous star, but I'm not sorry about choosing Tracy and baseball over the theater this year. Mom won't pay for theater school again, but I can probably join the drama club when I get to middle school.

I think that I got good at baseball because Tracy and I practiced together so much, and that Ilaria learned to speak English because she practiced it so much with me. Both make me proud.

Over the summer I think I'll practice gardening with Grandma (Tracy's dad rototilled a patch of the back yard for her). I think I'll also practice Spanish with Ilaria and try skateboarding with Tracy, too.

In fourth grade I learned how to memorize, I made some good friends, and I understood that practice really makes you better at every endeavor.

Sincerely,

Me (Sarah - not a star yet, but good at some endeavors)

The End

Glossary

The words and definitions in this glossary apply to the context of their use in Fourth Grade Began with Betrayal

Abridged - shorter and easier version

Abstract - something that doesn't portray realistic people, places, or things

Accolade - praise, cheer, applause, award

Ad lib - unplanned speech or actions (made up as you go along)

Adept - skilled, good at something

Akimbo - hands on hips with elbows sticking out

Align - in agreement or arranged in a straight line

Alternating - every other one, taking turns

Anguish - great pain or unhappiness

Anticipate - to expect or look forward to

Anxiety - worry, nervousness, stress

Arduous - difficult, hard, requiring a lot of effort

Aroma - good smell, scent

Astonish - really surprise

Bedraggled - sloppy and dirty

Betray - to not be loyal

Bizarre - strange and unusual

Boomeranged - flew around and returned in an out of control way

Brim - the very top edge of a container

Buckle down - get to work without getting distracted or delayed

Bungle - to do something in a clumsy way and mess it up

Compassion - concerned feelings for someone who is suffering

Confide - to tell someone a secret and trust them to not tell others

Cringe - show fear by bending your head and pulling your body inward

Cue - a signal to begin your turn

Cyst - a growth or lump that doesn't belong in a healthy body

Decibel - a unit of measure for sound volume

Declaration - a statement or announcement

Despite - even though

Diaphragm - a muscle used in breathing

Diplomat - a person that can deal with others in a sensitive way

Disprove - to prove that something is not true

Down port - people in areas of Suffolk County, NY refer to the village of Port Jefferson as "down port" (words and phrases used only in a certain region are called colloquialisms)

Drape - to arrange fabric loosely on or around something

Dusk - the evening time between daylight and darkness

Dutch door - a door that can be opened just on the top half or bottom half

Dwindle - gradually getting smaller

Effective - successfully getting the desired results

Effusive - warmly expressing feelings of pleasure, no holding back!

Elaborate - to add great detail and possibly exaggeration

Elegant - graceful and stylish

Embedded - pressed deeply into

Emerge - come out, begin to show

Encased - in a container

Encore - to perform again, usually called for by the audience

Endeavor - work to achieve a goal

Enhance - to make something better

Enlist - convince someone to participate or help out

Enrichment - improvement (in this story - more challenging assignments)

Enthusiastic - showing eager interest and enjoyment

Envelop - to surround completely

Essence - true character or quality

Euphoric - intense excitement and happiness

Exhilarating - thrilling

Expand - make larger or go further

Exquisite - extremely beautiful and delicate

Extracurricular - learning activities in addition to regular school

Feud - a long-running conflict or argument

Filter - a screen that can separate solids and liquids

Flaunt - show off to impress others

Flub - mess up

Fluster - to make nervous

Furthermore - besides, in addition (and another thing!)

Furtive - in a sneaky way

Galvanize - to excite someone into taking action

Glammed - to make oneself look glamorous

Glaze - to look uninterested

Gnarly - twisted

Grimace - ugly facial expression of disgust or pain

Grounded - not allowed to play with others or participate in fun activities

Haughty - act snobby and superior

Headline - large, bold newspaper heading that catches a readers' attention

Heartwarming - something nice that makes one feel loving and good

Humanity - caring for others

Humerus bone - the long bone in your upper arm

Humiliating - causing someone to feel ashamed by hurting their self-respect

Hurtle - to move at great speed

Hypothesis - an idea to be tested with the scientific method

Immerse - deeply involve

Immobile - not moving, not able to move

Imperious - acting powerful as if you are better than others

Impression - an opinion about someone or something

Impromptu - unplanned activity

Improvisation - dramatic interaction between characters without a script

In concert - working together

Incredulous - amazed and unable to believe something

Index finger - the finger next to the thumb

Indignant - being angry or annoyed because you've been insulted

Influence - affect someone so that they believe or behave in a certain way

Infuse - to insert one thing into something else so that it mixes in

Initiative - an effort to make something happen

Inquire - ask a question

Insight - able to understand deep meaning

Interpreter - someone that helps people of different languages communicate with each other

Interval - the amount of time between events

Intimidate - to make someone feel insecure or afraid

Intonation - the pattern or tone in which someone speaks

Kibosh - prevent in a "no way!" manner

Landlord - person who owns a building and is paid rent by the people using it

Launch - to put something in motion, get it going

Logic - way of thinking that makes sense

Matter of factly - attitude that something is obvious

Meander - to wander around slowly, not going directly toward something

Meld - put things together so that they become one thing

Melodic - like music that is pleasant to hear

Memoir - a story made from memories

Mesmerize - to hold someone's complete attention or to hypnotize

Miasma - a very unpleasant atmosphere

Mimic - to act like/copy someone or something else

Misery - a feeling of great discomfort and unhappiness

Mock - to make fun of, usually by imitating in an unattractive way

Momentum - power/force of movement

Monologue - a speech by one person

Mosaic - a picture or pattern made from small pieces that fit together like a puzzle

Muffle - to make something quieter

Mutter - to speak unclearly in a quiet voice

Observation - something you notice

Optional - not required

Ottoman - a piece of furniture for putting your feet up on

Palpable - plainly able to be heard, seen, or touched

Pantomime - acting like you are doing something, without sound or props

Peasants - in olden times: poor, uneducated farmers

Perception - idea or awareness

Perplexed - confused, baffled

Posture - how you hold your body (for example: slouching or reclining)

Prescribe - a rule, plan, or script

Projecting - speaking loudly enough to be heard in a large space, without yelling

Prompt - to quietly remind someone of what they are supposed to do

Rapt - fascinated

Rattletrap - old, rickety vehicle

Read cold - to read aloud without reading silently first

Regale - to entertain or amuse with talk

Reluctant - to do something you don't really want to do

Rep - representative

Repartee - quick, amusing comments and replies

Resent - to feel angrily envious

Revise - make changes

Revue - a show with many short, different parts

Rift - a serious break, crack, or split

Rototill - break up and turn soil with a rototiller machine

Routine - a series of activities that are followed regularly

Saturate - thoroughly soak

Secondhand - owned by someone else first

Sequence - in a certain order

Shimmer - shine with a soft, slightly moving light

Significant - important for a reason

Simmer - almost boiling hot, but not quite

Sing-song - saying something in obnoxious, repetitive tone

Snub - ignore or reject

Solitude - being alone (but not necessarily feeling lonely)

Sorry state - in poor condition

Spectator - someone who watches an event

Spike - suddenly rising up to a high point

Splay - spread out

Spotting - assisting someone who is attempting a gymnastic stunt

Stage chemistry - how well actors work together on stage

Stage whisper - a whisper loud enough to be heard throughout a theater

Stance - the position of feet and body to get ready for a particular movement

Start - a sudden surprise, something that startles a person

Stock market - where people buy and sell shares (little parts) of businesses

Stray - to go where it doesn't belong, like out of bounds

Subside - to become quiet and less active

Subtlety - without being obvious, loud, or noticeable

Surface - the top layer

Surge - a strong, swelling wave

Swaddle - wrap tightly, like a burrito or a baby in a blanket

Tactic - a plan or procedure to get a certain result

Talent scout - a person that finds performers for shows

Taunt - to sarcastically make fun of someone

Thrift shop - a store that sells used items

Tremble - to shake, usually from being nervous or afraid

Trinket - a small, cute, cheap item

Twilight - the time of day after the sun sets but it isn't nighttime yet

Unison - saying or singing the same thing at the same time

Velveteen - fabric that is like thin velvet

Warbly - a voice that sounds like it's shaking or vibrating

Made in the USA
Las Vegas, NV
19 September 2021